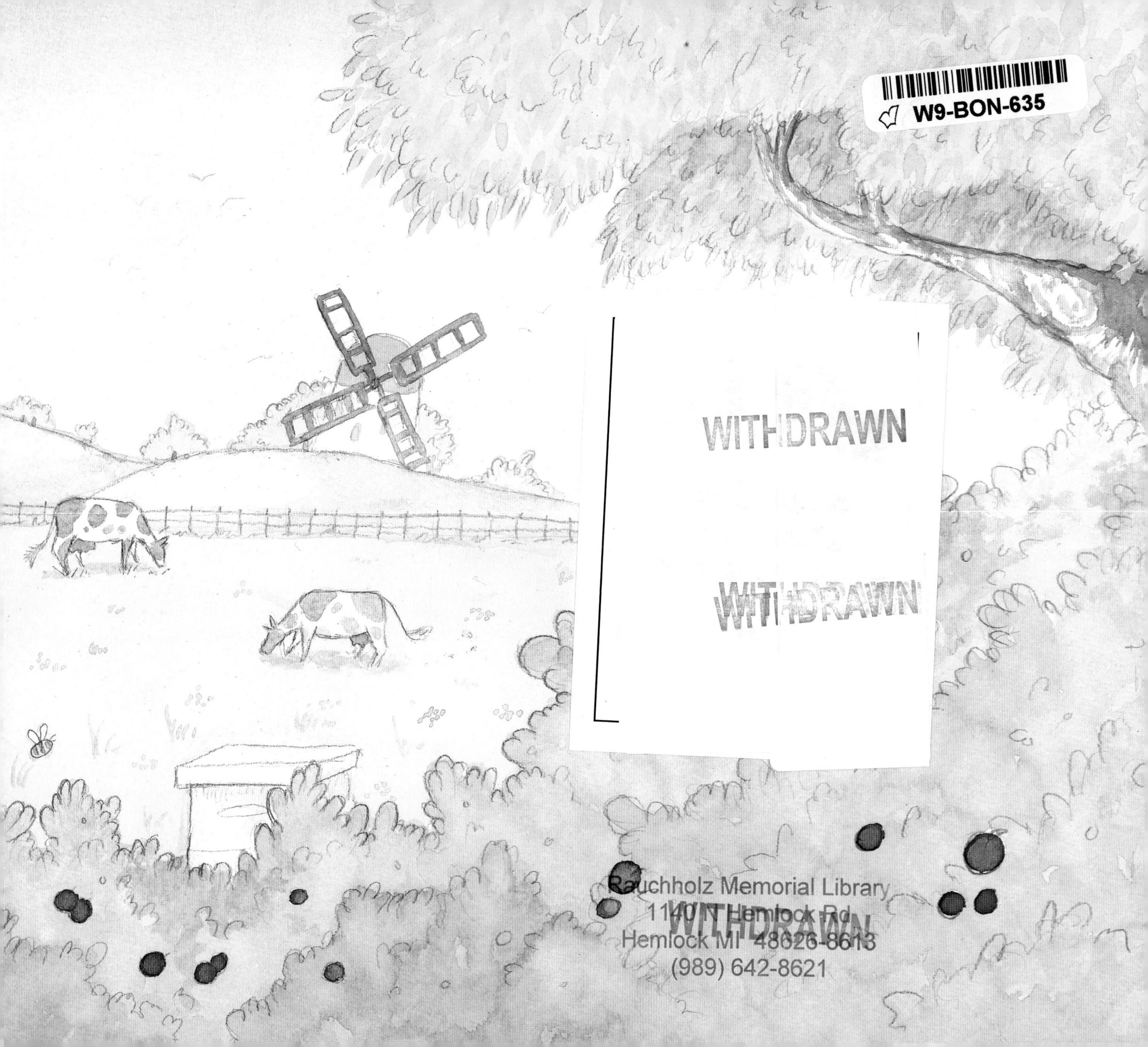

To my mother, who taught me how to bake –*C.P.*

For Mum and Dad, with a little bit of love –*H.W.*

tiger tales

an imprint of ME Media, LLC

202 Old Ridgefield Road, Wilton, CT 06897

Published in the United States 2011

Text copyright © 2011 Cynthia Platt

Illustrations copyright © 2011 Hannah Whitty

CIP data is available

Hardcover ISBN-13: 978-1-58925-095-6

Hardcover ISBN-10: 1-58925-095-8

Paperback ISBN-13: 978-1-58925-426-8

Paperback ISBN-10: 1-58925-426-0

Printed in China

LPP0710

For more insight and activities, visit us at www.tigertalesbooks.com

A Little Bit of Love

by Cynthia Platt

Illustrated by Hannah Whitty

tiger tales

One warm, bright day, a small mouse was feeling a little bit hungry.

"Mama," she said, "I need something to nibble."

"Of course, my little curly tail!" replied her mama mouse. "I have some lovely cheese for you."

"Oh, Mama, we always eat cheese. There's nothing lovely about cheese."

"I saved some crumbs for you," said the mama mouse.

The small mouse thought a moment. "No, I don't think it is crumbs that I crave. I need something sweet and new to nibble."

"Hmm," said the mama mouse. "I know just the thing!"

"You do, Mama?" asked the small mouse eagerly.

"Oh, yes. It's a special treat made of a little bit of love.
But to make it, we need to gather the ingredients."

"First, we need to visit
the beehives," said the
mama mouse.

"But you said the treat will be made of love, Mama. The bees certainly won't give us any love!" declared the small mouse.

"Oh, but the bees work patiently to gather pollen and make honey." said the mama mouse. "A lot of love goes into that kind of patience."

The small mouse took out a jar from her basket and let the honey *drip, drip, drop* right into it.

"My thanks, dear friends," the mama
mouse called to the buzzing bees.

"Where are we going next, Mama?" asked
the small mouse.

"We must get flour from the mill, my little
velvet ears!" said the mama mouse.

The small mouse frowned. "Now, Mama,
the flour can't *really* have love in it, can it?"

"The miller works hard
to grind wheat into flour,"
replied the mama mouse.
"When you work that hard,
you surely put some love
into it."

Together, they filled a little sack with
flour from underneath the mill's floor.

"Are we going home now, Mama?" asked the small mouse.

"Not yet, my little fuzzy coat. We need huckleberries."

"Huckleberries aren't made of love," said the small mouse.

"They're just made of . . . *berries!*"

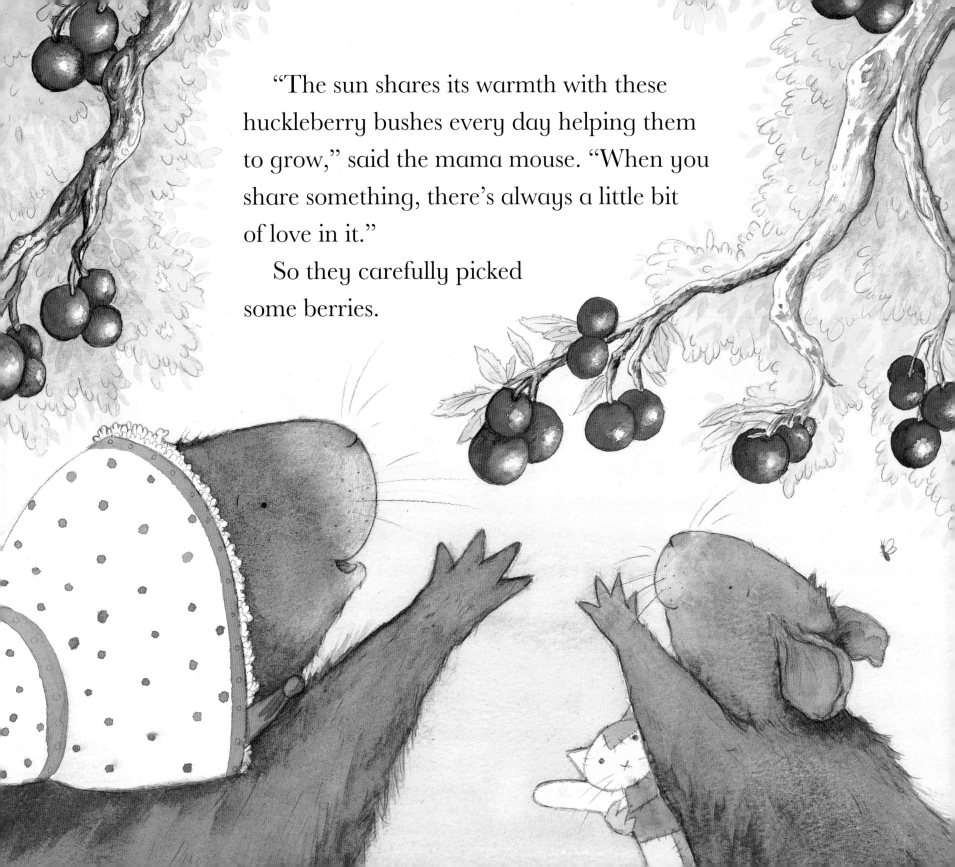

"The sun shares its warmth with these huckleberry bushes every day helping them to grow," said the mama mouse. "When you share something, there's always a little bit of love in it."

So they carefully picked some berries.

"My basket's getting heavy," said the small mouse, sounding just a little tired.

"We're almost done, my little pink nose. We just need sweet cream from the dairy," said the mama mouse.

The small mouse sighed. "I can't see how cream can be made of love, Mama."

"The cows make milk and cream for their calves,"
said the mama mouse. "When you make something for
your little one, it's always made of love."
She filled a jar with warm, sweet cream.

"Thank you, my dear," the
mama mouse said to the cow,
who nodded in return.

By now, the small mouse was very hungry indeed. She was
also very curious about what her mama was going to make.
"First, we put the flour into a bowl," said the mama mouse.
Tiny puffs of flour filled the air.

"Next, we shake the cream to make sweet butter,"
said the mama mouse.

With a *shake, shake, shake,* they added the butter, too.

"What's next, Mama?" asked the small mouse.

"Why, the honey, of course!" said the mama mouse.
She poured a tiny bit, *drip, drip, drop*, into the bowl.
The air smelled like sugar and flowers.

The small mouse looked into the bowl. "It doesn't look like something to nibble, Mama."

"Never you fear, my bright-eyed mouse."

Together, they mixed
up a dough . . .

rolled it as thin as a crumb, and
lifted it into a clay pan.

They poured the berries into
the pan, and placed another
layer of dough on top of it.

The small mouse smiled. "I know what we're
making now, Mama! It's a huckleberry pie."

"You guessed it!" said the mama mouse.

"But Mama," the small mouse said. "There's
one thing I still don't understand."

"What's that, my velvet tail?"

"Well, I see how the bees, the miller, the sun, and the cow all put love into this pie, but . . . are *you* going to put love into it, too?"

"Yes!" the mama mouse said. "There's love in patiently gathering ingredients, in working hard to create the pie, and in sharing it with you. But most of all, there's love in making something for my little one."

With that, she bent down, sealed the
pie with a kiss, and slid it into the oven.

In no time at all, it was done.

"Here is something sweet and new to eat," said the mama mouse. "Made with a little bit of love."

"I love our pie, Mama, and I love you!"

"I love you, too, my dear little mouse!" said the mama mouse.

And together, they feasted on every last nibble.